THE CUT-UPS CARRY ON

JAMES MARSHALL

PUFFIN BOOKS

with love
Ishaan

For Jeffrey Hillock and John Carlton

PUFFIN BOOKS
Published by the Penguin Group
Penguin Books USA Inc., 375 Hudson Street, New York, New York 10014, U.S.A.
Penguin Books Ltd, 27 Wrights Lane, London W8 5TZ, England
Penguin Books Australia Ltd, Ringwood, Victoria, Australia
Penguin Books Canada Ltd, 10 Alcorn Avenue, Toronto, Ontario, Canada M4V 3B2
Penguin Books (N.Z.) Ltd, 182–190 Wairau Road, Auckland 10, New Zealand

Penguin Books Ltd, Registered Offices: Harmondsworth, Middlesex, England

First published in the United States of America by Viking Penguin,
a division of Penguin Books USA Inc., 1990
Published in Puffin Books, 1993

1 3 5 7 9 10 8 6 4 2

LIBRARY OF CONGRESS CATALOGING-IN-PUBLICATION DATA
Marshall, James, 1942–
The Cut-ups carry on / James Marshall.   p.   cm.
Summary: Spud and Joe are forced by their mothers to take ballroom
dancing lessons and scheme to win a contest on television.
ISBN: 0-14-050726-4
[1. Dancing—Fiction.   2. Contests—Fiction.   3. Humorous
stories.]   I. Title.
PZ7.M35672Cut   1993   [E]—dc20   92-40721   CIP   AC

Printed in the United States of America
Set in Aster

Spud Jenkins and Joe Turner, a couple of true cut-ups,
just didn't know when to keep quiet.
"Our teacher this year is a real amateur," said Spud.
"She doesn't even believe in homework!"
"Think of all the free time we'll have!" said Joe.
The next day, the boys got a little surprise.

"*Dance class*!" cried Spud and Joe.

"You mean with *girls*?!"

"I'd rather eat bugs!" said Joe.

"Now, now," said his mom.

"I'm *sure* I'm having a heart attack,"
said Spud.
"How you boys carry on," said his mom.
"You can't *make* us go," said Joe.

That same afternoon Spud and Joe
went to their first dance class.
"We've been friends for years and years," said Joe.
"And we've been through a lot.
But this is the very worst."
"It'll be okay," said Spud.
"As long as we stick together."
"I hope the other guys don't see us," said Joe.

But the other guys were in dance class too.
"What a sorry-looking bunch," said Mr. MacKenzie.
"I can already spot a couple of cut-ups,"
said his wife.

"Look," said Spud. "There's Mary Frances Hooley.
Her mom probably made her come."
"I *love* dancing," said Mary Frances.
"And I'm *very* good."

The MacKenzies demonstrated a few flashy steps
for the boys and girls.

"They'll never get *me* to do that!" said Spud.
Mr. MacKenzie, who'd been teaching kids to dance
for years and years, spoke to the boys.

"Everybody knows that athletes
make the best dancers," he said.

But that little trick didn't work with Spud and Joe.
They didn't like dancing one bit.
"You're not trying," said Mrs. MacKenzie.

On the way home from dance class,
something interesting occurred.
Captain Kideo was on the air.
"Now remember, boys and girls,"
the Captain was saying, "the big talent contest
takes place on tomorrow's show.
And the first prize is your very own lunar walker,
just like the Captain's.
So come to the studio and perform on television—
and win the big prize!"
Mary Frances, Spud, and Joe stopped in their tracks.
"Did you hear *that*?" cried Mary Frances.

"If I don't get that lunar walker
I'll just *die*!" cried Mary Frances.
"I've *always* needed one," said Joe.
"The kids at school will be green with envy,"
said Spud.

"But what can we *do* in the contest?" said Joe.

"I wish I'd taken piano lessons," said Spud.

Mary Frances wasn't the least bit concerned.

"Well, *I* will do ballroom dancing," she said.

"And naturally I will win.

Of course I'll need a partner. . ."

Spud and Joe fell all over themselves.
"*I'll* be your partner!" cried Spud.
"No, *me!*" cried Joe. "I'm a better dancer!"

"You are *not!*" cried Spud.
"I'll make my choice tomorrow," said Mary Frances.
And they all went their separate ways.

That evening, in the privacy of his own room,
Joe practiced some dance steps with his cat
Fleabag Willie.
"She's just got to pick me!" said Joe.

Meanwhile at the Jenkins house, Spud and his mother
were spinning around the kitchen.
"Isn't this *fun*?" said Mrs. Jenkins.
"Faster, Mom, faster!" cried Spud.

On the morning school bus Spud and Joe
pretended not to see each other.
"That's odd," said the bus driver.
"They're usually as thick as thieves."
Suddenly a sports car roared into view.
It was Mary Frances, on her way to St. Bridget's School.

With her was the awful Charles Andrew Frothingham.
"I've decided that Charles Andrew will be my partner
in the big talent contest," called out Mary Frances.
Charles Andrew looked smug.
"But, but . . . !" cried Spud and Joe.
And Mary Frances was gone.

Spud and Joe staggered out of the bus.
In school they behaved like zombies.

"That's odd," said their teacher, Miss Ditswater.
"They're usually up to *something*."
"We'll never get that lunar walker now," said Joe.
At home the boys lay around like sick cats.

It was pitiful to see.

"Is something wrong?" asked Mrs. Turner.

Joe explained the problem.

"And the contest is in two hours!"

"Well," said Joe's mom. "There *is* a possible solution.
But there's no time to lose!"

Mrs. Turner banged out tunes on the piano.
And Mrs. Jenkins showed Spud how to follow.
"Why can't I lead?" said Spud.
"Hush up and dance," said his mom.

Spud and Joe gave it their all.
"Not bad," said Mrs. Jenkins. "Now for a costume."

"We can use one of my old wigs!" said Mrs. Turner.
Mrs. Jenkins got out her lipstick, eye shadow,
blusher, and false eyelashes.
"Now don't move!" she said.

"This better be worth it," said Spud.
"Hurry!" cried Mrs. Jenkins.

Spud and Joe rushed off to the television studio.
At the corner of Elm and Pine they ran into
their old friend Principal Lamar J. Spurgle
and his repulsive dog Bessie.
"Haven't I seen you someplace before,
young lady?" said Spurgle.
"Impossible," said Joe. "She's from out of state."
And the boys hurried on.
Lamar J. Spurgle, who never forgot a face,
was confused.

At the TV studio, Mary Frances and Charles Andrew
were just finishing up a dazzling tango.
The audience applause meter was going
simply berserk!

"I think we have our first prize winners!"
said Captain Kideo.
"Wait!" cried Joe. You haven't seen *us* yet!"
"Oh, very well," said the Captain. "But make it snappy."

Spud and Joe danced their hearts out.

"I've seen chickens dance better than *that*!"

whispered Charles Andrew.

"They're no competition for *us*," said Mary Frances.

When Spud and Joe were finished dancing,

and the applause had died down,

Captain Kideo announced the winners.

Spud Jenkins and Joe Turner won second prize.

"Holy smoke!" cried Spud.

"Two tickets to the Astrojets game!"

They couldn't have been more thrilled.

"And the first prize winners are . . ." called out Captain Kideo,

"Mary Frances Hooley and Charles Andrew Frothingham!"

"This isn't at *all* what I had in mind!"
said Mary Frances. "Maybe we can trade it
for those Astrojet tickets."

But Spud and Joe were already heading for home—
and dancing all the way.